What Am I Worth?

What Am I Worth?

Written by
Mark Januszewski
Illustrated by Aaron Jones

What Am I Worth?
Copyright © 2018 by Mark Januszewski
www.MarkJBooks.com

All rights reserved. No part of this publication may be reproduced, distributed, or transmitted in any form or by any means, including photocopying, recording, or other electronic or mechanical methods, without the prior written permission of the publisher, except in the case of brief quotations embodied in critical reviews and certain other noncommercial uses permitted by copyright law. For permission requests, write to the publisher, addressed "Attention: Permissions Coordinator" at info@markjbooks.com

Quantity sales special discounts are available on quantity purchases by corporations, associations, and others. For details, contact the publisher at the address above.

Orders by U.S. trade bookstores and wholesalers. Email info@markjbooks.com

For more information info@markjbooks.com
The Author can be reached directly at MarkJBooks.com

Artwork & overall Design by Aaron Jones. For more information contact this artist at boldtruthbooks@yahoo.com

10 9 7 8 0 5 7 8 2 1

ISBN 978-0-578-21309-5

To the great men who raised me, Uncle Dan and Uncle Mo.

They taught me peace and love coupled with gratitude will make a person priceless.

Once upon a time in a small town in western Africa a brother and sister were having an argument

They were twins. The boy's name was Udo and the girl's name was Funanya.

"You are even not worth one dollar," Udo shouted at his sister Funanya.

"Oh yeah," she yelled back, "Well, you're not worth 10 cents!"

Udo started to cry because his feelings were hurt. Then Funanya started to cry too.

But they kept yelling at each other.

"You are not worth 5 cents," the brother screamed and the sister said, "You are not worth one penny."

And they both cried even more.

Udo said, "Let's go ask Grandfather, then you'll know I am worth more than you."

And Funanya said, "OK but Grandfather will tell you I'm worth more than you," and they agreed to go ask the Grandfather.

And so they walked in silence to the home of Grandpa Bongani. And the Grandfather was very happy to see the twins. He hugged Udo and Funanya and their tears stopped.

"We came so you would settle our argument," Funanya said. "What are we worth?"

And Grandfather nodded and said, "What a person is worth is an important question. Would you both like to discover what you are worth?"

Both Udo and Funanya shouted "YES!" at the same time.

And the Grandfather stood up and walked into another room. He came back with a pretty stone in his hand. "Do you remember this stone?" he asked.

And then the Grandfather said, "Bring it to the marketplace and hold it before you. If someone asks you about the stone do not say anything. Simply hold up two fingers. If they say they want it and give you money, tell them you must talk to your Grandfather first and hurry right home. Do you understand?"

"Yes Grandfather. Just hold up 2 fingers and if they want to pay for the stone, tell them we must ask you first." And as they left, the Grandfather said, "Peace be the journey." He touched his heart and then opened his arms and hands.

And so Udo and Funanya headed to the marketplace. When they arrived, Udo held the pretty stone in front of himself. There were many people wandering in the marketplace looking at foods, fruits, spices, clothes and flowers.

A woman in a blue shirt and yellow shorts stopped by the children and said, "My that is a beautiful stone. I would like it in my garden. How much does it cost?"

Funanya did what Grandfather Bongani had told her. She held up two fingers. The woman got a big smile on her face and said, "Wow, two dollars! I gladly give you two dollars." She reached into her pink purse and took out two dollars.

"We have to talk to our Grandfather first," said Funanya said. She and Udo ran quickly to his home and were very excited when they told him what happened.

Then Grandfather said, "Now take the stone to the museum and hold the stone before you like before. If anyone asks about it, say nothing. Just hold up two fingers."

And as they left, the Grandfather said, "Peace be the journey". He touched his heart and then opened his arms and hands.

Udo held up two fingers.

"Oh, my! That is a wonderful price. I will be most happy to pay you two thousand dollars for your stone!" Udo said, "We have to ask our Grandfather first."

Udo and Funanya were so happy they ran to the home. They ran so fast they did not notice the flowers on the road or the giraffes and the elephants on the hill. When they told him about the man willing to pay two thousand dollars, the Grandfather again said nothing about the money.

"Now I want you to go to the building where all jewelers work. Again, be silent, just hold the stone before you. If anyone asks about it, just hold up two fingers like before."

And as they left, the Grandfather said, "Peace be the journey." He touched his heart and then opened his arms and hands.

Udo and Funanya went to the jeweler's building quickly but again they were silent. Neither could understand why their Grandfather was not excited about the two thousand dollars the man wanted to pay for the sparkly stone.

The twins walked into the jeweler's building and held the stone before them. Soon a woman with a grand smile in a red dress asked them if they were selling the stone. Funanya held up two fingers.

The woman yelled loudly, "I have never seen a stone like this, it is so rare and so big and beautiful. I will be happy to pay you two-hundred thousand for it right now!"

And Funanya said, "We have to talk to our Grandfather first." And they left the big building.

They ran back to the house even faster this time. They told the Grandfather about the large fortune the woman wanted to pay for the stone.

"Do you think your brother's life is more valuable than that stone?" asked the Grandfather.

"Yes," said Funanya. "Then tell him," said the Grandfather. Funanya said, "Udo, you are worth more than the stone."

"Does that feel good Udo?" asked the Grandfather. "Yes" Udo said. "You will make your life more valuable by telling Funanya the same thing," said the Grandfather. And Udo told his twin sister she was worth far more than a stone.

"And do you both know that what you are saying to each other is true?" The twins both said "yes" at the same time. "And do you both feel more valuable and treasured now?"

And the twins smiled and shouted "yes!" And the grandfather said, "the stone cannot decide where to place itself, but you can decide where to place yourself. The stone will never know what it is worth. Others will decide its value."

And Udo asked, "Will others decide what we are worth like the stone?" "No," said the grandfather, "if you let others determine your worth you will be like a stone and you will never know your real value. You must learn to see your own worth, that you are priceless"

And Udo asked, "How do we do that grandfather?"

"To know in your heart that you are priceless, worth far more than 100 stones, and no longer need to let others determine your value is easy and wonderful," said the Grandfather.

And then the grandfather said, "You become more and more valuable by making others feel more valuable." And the twins asked "Do we tell others they are more valuable than 100 stones?"

And Grandfather Bongani smiled and shook his head "no." Then he said, "The two greatest things to feel are love and peace. The more love and peace you give to others, the more love and peace will grow in you."

Then he said, "When you feel love and peace growing, you will know you are priceless." And Funanya asked, "Is that why you always say 'Peace Be The Journey' to everyone Grandfather Bongani?" And the grandfather said yes.

And then Udo asked, "Why do you touch your heart and open your arms when you say Peace Be The Journey?"

"There is One Love that runs through everyone's heart. Sometimes people forget that so I touch my heart and open my arms to share that One Love with others and hope they feel love again."

"Peace and love are twins. Where there is peace, there is love. And where there is love, there is peace. Peace and love are twins, just like Udo and Funanya are twins. It is why we picked those names for you."

"What do you mean Grandfather Bongani?" Funanya asked. "Udo, your name means love and Funanya your name means peace." And the twins smiled.

"But what if we are not together?" Udo asked. "Is there a way to always keep peace and love together Grandfather Bongani?"

"Yes there is. Gratitude is like a rope that can never break and keeps Love and Peace together.

That is why my father named me Bongani. It means Gratitude."

And with a big smile Udo shouted, "So my name means Love, my sister's name means Peace and your name means Gratitude!"

And all three felt priceless as Peace and Love ran into the arms of Gratitude.

Other books by the Author

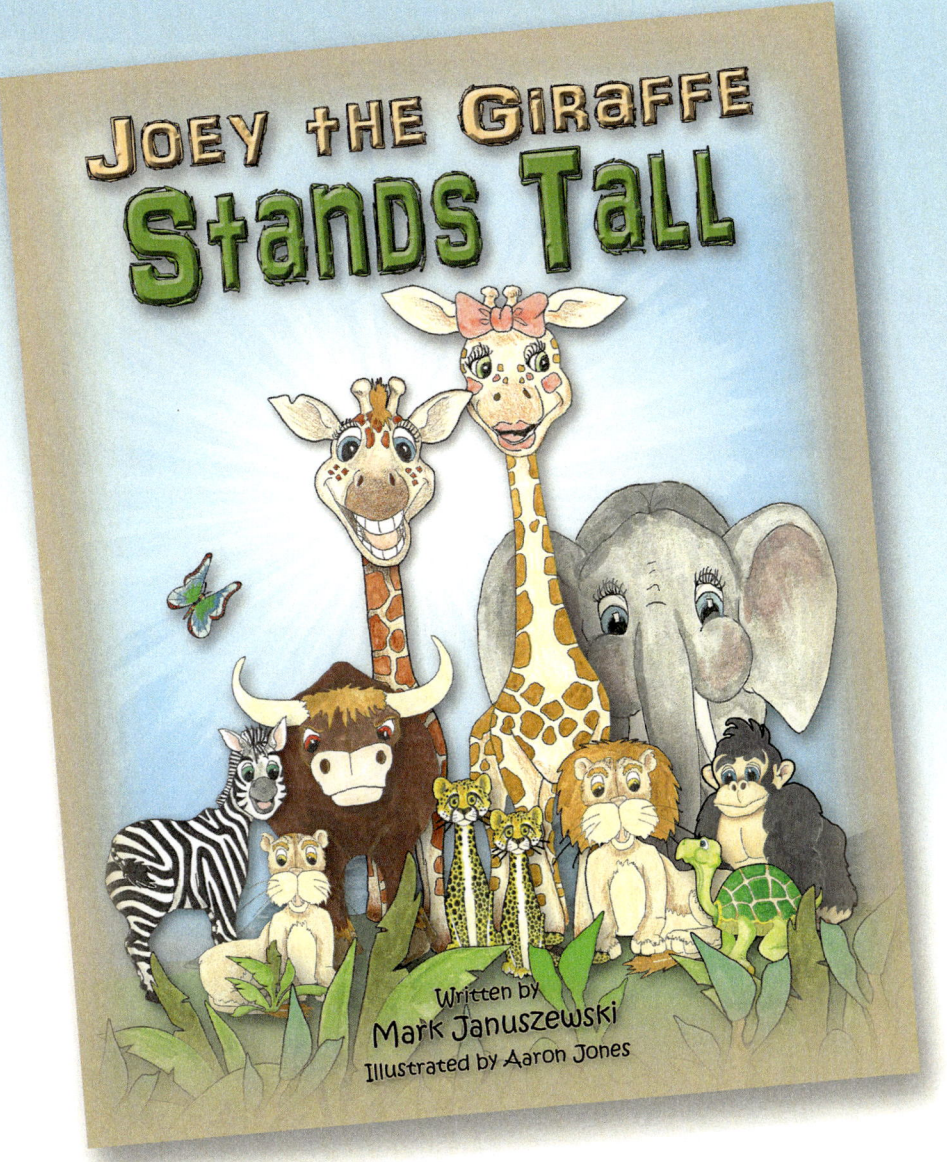

Available at markjbooks.com and Amazon.com

Other books by the Author

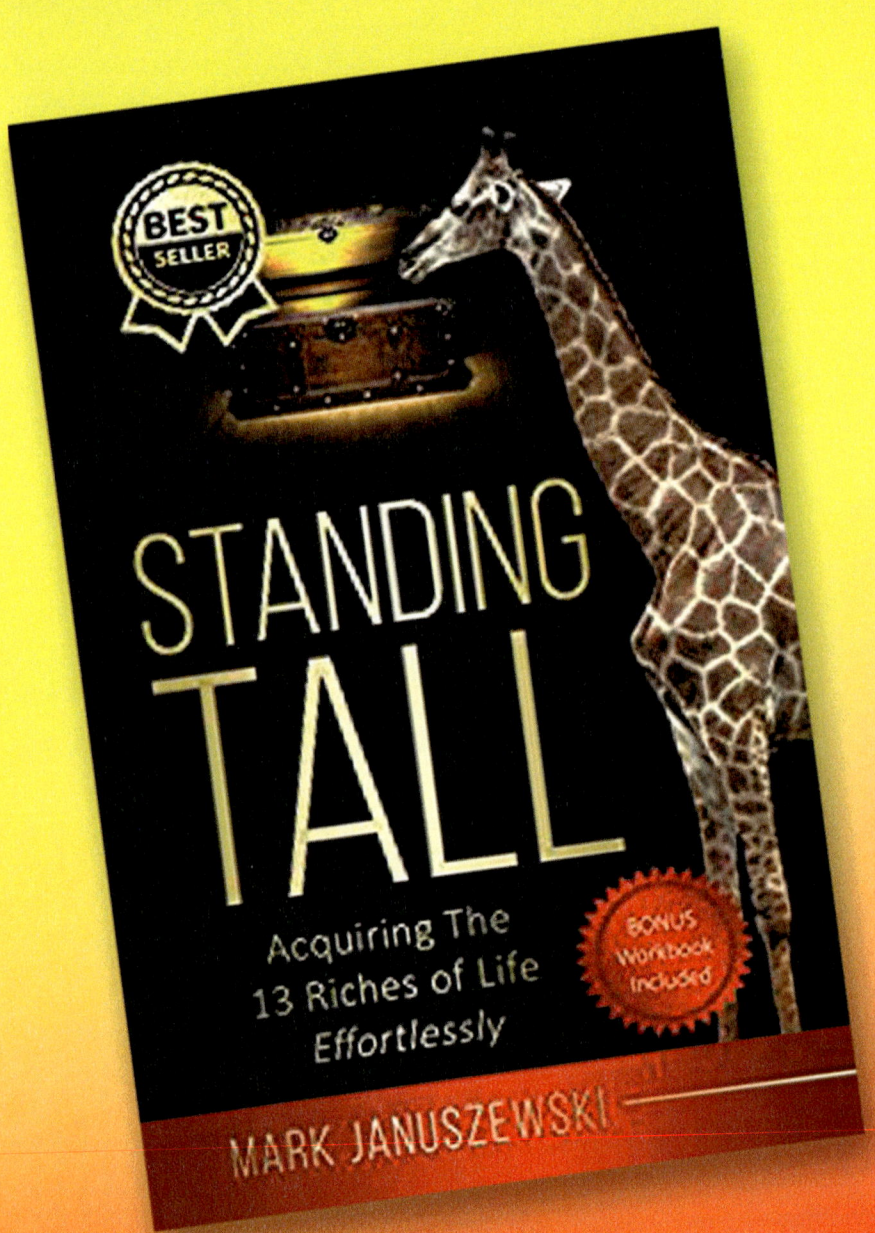

Available at markjbooks.com and Amazon.com

Made in the USA
San Bernardino, CA
03 March 2019